PLACER COUNTY
6600167
D0601916

Sam's Winter Hat

To the memory of my dear
friend Billy Miller
—Albert Lamb

For Albert and Popsy and
all with love
—David McPhail

Library of Congress Cataloging-in-Publication Data
Lamb, Albert.
Sam's winter hat / by Albert Lamb ; illustrated by David McPhail.
p. cm.
"Cartwheel books."
Summary: Sam, a forgetful young bear, loses his special new, blue, woolly hat and finds it in a surprising location.
ISBN 0-439-79304-1
[1. Bears—Fiction. 2. Lost and found possessions—Fiction. 3. Hats—Fiction.] I. McPhail, David, 1940- ill. II. Title.
PZ7.L1597Sam 2006
[E]--dc22
2005018720

ISBN: 0-439-79304-1

10 9 8 7 6 5 4 3 2 1 6 7 8 9 10/0

Printed in Singapore 46
First printing, October 2006

Sam's Winter Hat

By Albert Lamb
Pictures by David McPhail

SCHOLASTIC INC.

New York Toronto London Auckland Sydney
Mexico City New Delhi Hong Kong Buenos Aires

Sam Bear was going out to play with Billy, his next-door neighbor and best friend.

Mama Bear helped Sam put on his red winter coat.

Sam and Billy rode their tricycles around and around.

What they liked best was to bump into each other and crash!

"I'm getting hotter than a baked apple!" said Sam. And he took off his red winter coat.

"Where is your coat?" Mama Bear asked when Sam went inside for lunch.

"Oh, no!" he said. "I think I lost it!"

Just then, Billy came to the door.

"I've brought back Sam's red winter coat!"

"Lucky me!" said Sam.

The next day was even colder. Mama Bear helped Sam put on his red winter coat and his green fuzzy mittens.

"Will you look at the wheels on my tricycle!" said Sam when he got outside. "They've gone all wibbly wobbly!"

He pushed his tricycle into the garage and hit the wheel with a hammer to get the wobble out.

When he came in for lunch, Mama Bear asked him, "Where are your green fuzzy mittens?"

"Oh, no," said Sam. "I had them on a minute ago!"

Just then, Papa Bear came in with Sam's green mittens.

"Look what I found in the garage," he said.

"Lucky me!" said Sam.

The next day was the coldest yet.

Just as he was going out, a package arrived.

"It's for you, dear! From Grandma!" said Mama Bear.

“It’s a new blue woolly hat!” said Sam. “I’m going to keep it forever!”

Sam could hardly wait to show Billy his new hat.

So, instead of walking the long way around the fence, he climbed over it.

“Now I have a woolly hat like yours, Billy,” said Sam. “Except it’s blue!”

“Where is it?” asked Billy.

“Oh, no!” said Sam. “My whole life is going wobbly!”

Sam Bear tried very hard to remember

where he'd lost his new blue woolly hat.

Sam was trying so hard to remember that he fell over backward. Up in the tree above him, he saw his blue woolly hat.

"There it is!" said Sam. "Lucky me!"

Sam and Billy climbed the tree together in order to retrieve the hat.

Just then, it started to snow.

"It's good we have our woolly hats on," said Billy.

"It sure is!" said Sam, smiling his happiest smile. "Lucky us!"